R. J.

R. J. loves playing sports with her brothers. Her favorite sport is soccer, and she is one of the best players in the neighborhood. R. J. never plays with dolls or wears dresses. R. J. likes to act tough, but deep inside, she has a lot of fears—until she learns to pray about them!

Pi

Pi is smart and the quietest Fright sibling. He loves to paint and play the piano. When he is outdoors, his favorite thing to do is skateboard! Pi has a very kind heart. Sometimes he makes bad choices, but in the end he always does the right thing.

prayer monsters

Pi Fright Skates into Trouble
A Story about Integrity

created by Tracey Madder

illustrated by Bonnie Pang

Tyndale House Publishers, Inc.
Carol Stream, IL

Visit Tyndale's website for kids at www.tyndale.com/kids.

Visit Tracey Madder online at www.traceymadder.com.

TYNDALE is a registered trademark of Tyndale House Publishers, Inc. The Tyndale Kids logo is a trademark of Tyndale House Publishers, Inc.

The Prayer Monsters logo is a trademark of Super Faith, LLC.

Pi Fright Skates into Trouble: A Story about Integrity

Copyright © 2017 by Tracey Madder. All rights reserved.

Illustrations by Bonnie Pang. Copyright © by Tyndale House Publishers. All rights reserved.

Designed by Jacqueline L. Nuñez

Edited by Sarah Rubio

Scripture quotations are taken from the *Holy Bible*, New Living Translation, copyright © 1996, 2004, 2015 by Tyndale House Foundation. Used by permission of Tyndale House Publishers, Inc., Carol Stream, Illinois 60188. All rights reserved.

Pi Fright Skates into Trouble is a work of fiction. Where real people, events, establishments, organizations, or locales appear, they are used fictitiously. All other elements of the story are drawn from the author's imagination.

For manufacturing information regarding this product, please call 1-800-323-9400.

For information about special discounts for bulk purchases, please contact Tyndale House Publishers at csresponse@tyndale.com, or call 1-800-323-9400.

ISBN 978-1-4964-0870-9

Printed in China

23	22	21	20	19	18	17
7	6	5	4	3	2	1

To my husband, thank you for believing in me.
To my children, in memory of your summer lemonade stands.
T. M.

ACKNOWLEDGMENTS
A special thank you to my friends at Tyndale.

2

Pi Fright is no ordinary monster.

He lives in a tiny house at the end of Quiet Street.

3

But his family is not very quiet! Pi has two brothers and two sisters.

Pi is the oldest. Then comes Zeppi, then the two girls, R. J. and Tora, and finally baby Booyah.

Mom and Dad handle the whole crowd with a lot of laughter.

4

Pi loves to play the piano, ride his skateboard, and paint.

Today, Pi is painting some posters for Zeppi. Zeppi is hosting his basketball team's annual Spaghetti Stand Fund-raiser.

Pi finishes the posters and hands them to Zeppi. "Thanks!" Zeppi says. "The signs look super."

"You're welcome," says Pi, grabbing his skateboard. He runs to meet his friend Isaac.

Isaac doesn't have a skateboard, so Pi and Isaac take turns practicing the kickflip with Pi's board.

"I almost got it," Pi tells Isaac. "Just give me one more try." Pi has already had five tries. Isaac sighs and sits back down on the curb.

9

"You've got to see this!" yells Tommy, rushing out of his house. "I got it yesterday for my birthday. Isn't it great?"

The skateboard's glittery red paint sparkles in the sunlight.

"It's awesome," says Pi.

"Wow!" Isaac whispers.

Pi looks down at his old green skateboard.

"Check out the panther on the bottom," adds Tommy.

Tommy jumps on his new skateboard and zooms past Pi.

Then, Tommy lands a kickflip on the first try!

"Wow!" Isaac whispers again.

12

Pi hands his skateboard to Isaac and trudges toward the spaghetti stand.

"The sale is a huge success so far," Zeppi tells Pi. He holds up a jar full of cash. "It must be the great signs!" Zeppi smiles at his brother.

Pi smiles back and decides to help.

14

Zeppi places pasta into each customer's bowl, R. J. spoons on the sauce, and Tora sprinkles on the cheese. She says a quick blessing before sending each monster happily down the line. Booyah says, "Thank you"—or at least he tries. And Pi collects the money.

SPAGHETTI

As the last customer comes through the line, Pi looks down at the money jar in his hands and gets an idea.

16

"Where's he going?" Pi hears R. J. ask as he races down the street.

Pi gets back home just as Zeppi says, "Let's add up our grand total!" He reaches for the jar of money.

17

But the jar is empty! The money is gone!

The Frights search the spaghetti stand, but the money is nowhere to be found.

Zeppi's face turns red and sweat beads up on his forehead. "I think the money's been stolen!" he exclaims.

That night at dinner, Tora keeps staring at Pi. Pi stares at the table. It feels like he has a lump in his stomach. A lump as heavy and cold as a glass jar full of money.

When he goes to his room that night, Pi finds Tora sitting on his bed. "I think you might have gotten yourself into trouble today, Pi," she says. "God wants us to make good choices and do what is right."

Pi doesn't say anything. The lump in his stomach feels colder and heavier than ever.

"Can I teach you my Prayer for Good Choices?" Tora asks. "It's what I pray when I'm not sure what to do."

Pi nods. Together, they pray,

Lord, be with us both day and night.
Love and guide us to do what's right.
We praise you, Lord, in all we do.
We love you, Lord, and thank you too.
Amen.

21

The next morning, Pi confesses to Zeppi and his dad.

"I stole the money," Pi says. "I'm really sorry."

"Why would you do that?" Zeppi asks. "You know the team needs it."

"I took the money to buy this," Pi says. He shows Zeppi and Dad a skateboard.

The skateboard's glittery red paint sparkles in the sunlight.

"You'll have to return this skateboard. Stealing is never okay, son," Dad says.

"Dad, I want to try to make things right. What if—" Pi starts. He whispers the rest of his plan in his dad's ear.

Dad agrees to the plan. Dad gives Zeppi the money for the uniforms. Now Pi has to work to pay Dad back.

Pi works hard.

He mixes up four big batches of horn polish for his
babysitter, Gracie Claws, and her brother, Max.

He pulls piles of flowers from Tommy's weed garden.

And he gives baby Booyah a bath every day for a week. "Don't forget to shampoo the tip of his tail!" Mom reminds Pi.

At the end of the last bath, Pi is wet from head to toe. But he has finally earned enough money to pay Dad. Now he doesn't have to return the skateboard.

Pi grabs the board and heads out to play.

Tora follows. "I want to see how fast you go on your new skateboard," she says.

But Pi hands the skateboard to Isaac.

"This is for you," he says. "Now you don't have to wait for a turn anymore."

"Wow!" Isaac whispers.

Pi thanks God for helping him do what is right.

Then, he hops on his green skateboard and lands a kickflip on the first try!

This is what the LORD says:
"Be just and fair to all.
Do what is right and good."

Isaiah 56:1

30

Tora

Tora is the princess of the Fright family! She has perfect manners and loves to play with dolls. Tora also loves to tell her siblings what to do. Even though she can be bossy, Tora usually gives good advice. She always reminds her siblings to pray to God when they need help.